Adelyn's Adventure

IN
THE
GARDEN

Charles Bruckerhoff

Charles

Sequoia House Books™

Children's Books by the Author

Adelyn's Adventure:

In the Forest

In the Garden

On the Beach

Sequoia House Books™

Adelyn's Adventure is a children's book series
published by the author

For purchasing and reviews contact:
www.SequoiaHouseBooks.com
and booksellers in the United States of America
and the global market.

Images licensed by Shutterstock, Inc.

Cover design, book interior design, and typesetting by
Mario Lampic

Printed in the United States of America.

Library of Congress Control Number: 2022906765

ISBN 978-0-9905838-7-5

Second edition: April 2022

FOR

CHILDREN

PARENTS

AND GRANDPARENTS.

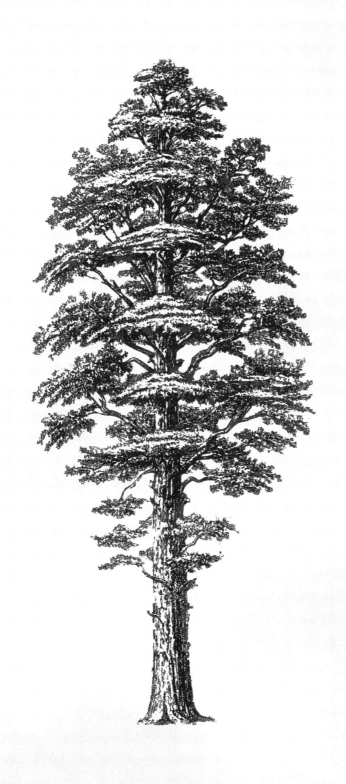

If you have a garden and a library,
you have everything you need.

— Cicero

Never bend your head. Always hold it high.
Look the world straight in the eye.

— Helen Keller

IN
THE
GARDEN

1

On a Saturday in the summertime, Adelyn was having dinner late in the evening with Grandmother and Grandfather at their home in the country.

Grandfather had barbecued beef ribs and, as a last touch before taking them off the grill, poured on a thick layer of his homemade BBQ sauce.

Grandmother steamed fresh corn on the cob and green peas. She also served cold pickled beets and a tossed salad of mixed lettuce leaves, sliced tomatoes and cucumbers.

During dinner, they talked about how pleasant the weather had been this summer.

"Weather forecast predicts a rainstorm, starting at 9:00 p.m., continuing to 7:00 a.m. tomorrow morning," Grandfather said.

"Perfect for the garden," Grandmother remarked.

"I picked our first ripe tomatoes today, just in time for Grandmother to add to our salad," Grandfather added.

Adelyn's grandparents loved to put in a garden every spring. It required hard work for part of almost every day.

They usually tended the garden in late afternoon when it was cool outside, and all their other work was done.

Dinner was late today, because they pulled weeds and hoed soil in the garden.

Adelyn's job was gathering up the weeds in Grandfather's oak wicker basket and dumping them into the compost bin.

"Store-bought vegetables are okay in winter when the garden stops producing. Fresh garden vegetables are much better tasting and better for your health," Grandfather said whenever table talk turned to gardening.

"Dinner was super scrumptious. So good," Adelyn said when she ate the last morsel on her plate. "When the rain stops tomorrow morning, my next adventure starts. I'm exploring the garden."

Grandmother leaned over with a napkin, smiling broadly, to wipe smudges of BBQ sauce from her cheeks.

"That's great news," Grandmother said. "You might find more tomatoes have ripened overnight. Pick them. Bush beans are also ripe. Pick a few handfuls and I'll cook them for dinner tomorrow. And cucumbers."

Adelyn yawned big and long. "Excuse me. I think I'll head upstairs now, go to bed and read my book. I'm really tired."

"You've worked hard, outside in the sunshine," Grandfather said. "With rain falling on the roof overnight, you'll sleep well and be ready for the adventure tomorrow."

Grandmother said, "Hoeing the bean patch wore me out. Grandfather and I will turn in early, too._

"Love you both. Good night."

"Good night. Love you, too. See you in the morning," Grandmother said.

She stood and pushed her chair to the table.

"I'll put away the dishes and clean up the table," Grandfather said.

Adelyn walked sleepily up the stairs, washed her hands and face, brushed her teeth, combed her hair and pulled on pajamas.

She turned back the covers, grabbed her book and crawled into bed.

Later on, Grandmother checked on her, as she did every night. She was already sound asleep, her book opened by her side.

Grandmother, smiling proudly, kissed Adelyn's forehead. She put the book on the nightstand, turned out the light and gently closed the door.

2

next morning, Adelyn awoke in silence.

The all-night rainstorm had just ended. She went to her bedroom window and opened it. Warm morning air flowed in gently.

She breathed in deep.

She shouted out the window, "The air is so fresh! It's sweet!"

In the distance, Crow answered with, "Caw, caw, caw-caw-caw! Good morning."

"Good morning to you, Crow! 'See more, do more, know more,'" she said, repeating Crow's advice from her last adventure.

Sunlight, streaming through light fog, turned rain drops on leaves and grass into tiny diamonds, and emeralds. "So beautiful!"

Her next thought was her adventure in the garden today.

"I have to get ready!"

She rushed to the bathroom, showered and brushed her teeth.

She dressed in faded green cotton shorts and a light yellow T-shirt with a green braid on the neck and sleeves. She pulled on white, ankle-length socks with a braided green trim.

After brushing her hair, she paused to look at herself in the mirror.

"You're a beautiful, clever little girl. Do the right thing, always. You will have fun, go places and do things. Now, get going!"

She did her dance routine in socks through the hallway and dashed downstairs.

From the kitchen, where Grandmother had been preparing breakfast, she heard Adelyn greet the splendid morning at her bedroom window.

"Sounds like you're ready for a new adventure. We have fruit, yogurt, orange juice and fresh-baked cornbread for breakfast," Grandmother said while placing them all on the kitchen table.

Grandfather grabbed a banana for breakfast early this morning. He went to town to get a haircut and shop for groceries. He'll be back at noon."

They both sat at the table.

"Eat plenty, so you're full of energy for the adventure."

"This might be my all-time favorite breakfast," Adelyn said, smelling the food on her plate. She took a bite of buttered cornbread. "Yum! Oh my, it's so good, Grandmother."

Within minutes, she finished eating and took her plate, cup and silverware to the sink.

She kissed Grandmother's cheek and hugged her tight.

"Thank you for making breakfast, Grandmother. I love you. Now, I'm going on my adventure in the garden, Grandmother. I'll pick the veggies you want for dinner."

"Have fun. I love you, too," Grandmother said, smiling with pride at her youthful gusto and good manners. She sat back to enjoy her cup of coffee, before going to work for the family business.

In the breezeway, Adelyn donned her blue and white polka-dotted hat and tied on her lime green sneakers.

She grabbed the handle of Grandfather's basket, opened the door and walked into the morning light.

10

Grandparents' garden was beyond the backyard, a short walk along a grassy path. The sun had not burned off the fog, making her walk on the pathway dreamlike, mystical.

Birds were chirping in the trees. A woodpecker was tat-tat-tat-tatting on a dead tree limb.

Chipmunk, sitting on the path in front of her, scurried away zigzaggedly. "Cluck- cluck-cluck, danger, danger." Bushy tail pointing up, it disappeared down a ground burrow.

"Kee-you! . . . Kee-you! . . . Kee-you! I see you," Hawk said, flying at tree-top level. "I plucked this trout from the river to feed my chicks. They're always starved. No time to visit now. Have a great day," Hawk added, winging hard and fast north, the trout gripped by Hawk's talons.

"You have a great day, too, Hawk."

3

At the garden entrance, Adelyn paused.

Years ago, Grandfather had designed the large garden in a half-moon shape with a fieldstone wall along the border.

He arranged spaces inside the garden to plant herbs, flowers and vegetables separately. Some plants he mixed together, he said, "because they're good neighbors."

At each tip of the half-moon, Grandfather placed a tall, rusted wrought iron arbor with a gate.

He said to her, "The arbor gate at the entrance welcomes all visitors to enjoy and work in the garden. If you take care of the garden, the garden takes care of you. At the other point, a second arbor gate wishes visitors farewell and safe travels."

From entrance arbor to exit arbor, Grandfather laid out a winding walkway paved with thick, heavy Belgian stones.

At the midpoint, he placed a compass rose with its face oriented to magnetic North.

One day last summer, Adelyn asked Grandfather about the compass rose.

He walked with her to the garden. They passed through the entrance gate and continued walking on the winding stone path until they arrived at the center of the garden.

"Here it is."

She crouched down to look at the large, cement disk laid in the stone path years ago. "It's very decorative, beautiful."

Feeling the surface with her fingers, she added, "There are eight raised points. Four marked with N, S, E, and W. And four with no letters."

"Good study," Grandfather said.

"The points with letters tell us the four cardinal directions, north, south, east and west. The other points are for directions in between."

Then, he told his reason for placing a compass rose in the center of their garden.

"Explorers in ancient times relied on tall trees or mountains in the distance, and stars in the night sky, to guide their long travels away from home and back again."

"Later on, more than two thousand years ago, the Chinese invented the magnetic compass, and that helped guide explorers."

Then, he explained how to use the compass.

"A traveler would talk through the process like this."

"I need to go to a town in that direction," while pointing there.

"I see no roads or signs showing how to get there.

"On the compass, what direction is that?

"The compass point, E, for east, points that way.

"Now, what landmark do I see in the east?

"A tall, round-top mountain.

"I will travel east to that mountain to get to the town, as long as I can see it.

"In the forest and at night, when I can't see the mountain, I will use the compass as a guide.

"That's how we use a simple compass today. To help guide our travel to a distant location.

"The GPS in our car is a modern compass. We tell it where we want to go. It shows us and tells us how to get there.

"The half moon is a sign of fertility, life and death. The compass rose is also a symbol, reminding us to seek guidance for important decisions in life.

"The winding stone path in this garden is our walk through life.

"We don't follow instinct, like the wild animals of the forest, we make decisions about what to do at every turn.

"We usually choose to do the right thing.

"Sometimes, we make mistakes. Everyone makes mistakes, because humans are not perfect.

"If we do a bad thing, like hurt somebody, we must right the wrong, help heal the wounds and ask for forgiveness.

"The compass rose reminds visitors to seek guidance and stay on the right path for a good life."

"That's what the Ten Commandments are for," she offered.

"Yes, Adelyn, and our Constitution and laws. You see the connection clearly."

The sun was setting.

"We should head back to the house. It'll be dark soon," Grandfather said.

Snapping back to the present, Adelyn recalled her plan for an adventure in the garden today.

And to pick vegetables for Grandmother.

She stood on the stone threshold of the entrance arbor gate.

Hundreds of radiant red clematis flowers were in full bloom. The bushy vines, leaves and flowers wildly overspread the arbor, top to bottom.

The garden was filled with lush plants. Flowers in full bloom, plants loaded with ripening fruits and vegetables, and herbs tall, bushy, fragrant.

"So well-tended," she said, thinking of her grandparents' hard work.

The warm overnight rain had blended the aromas of flowers, herbs and soil into Mother Nature's perfume.

Adelyn closed her eyes and sniffed the rich scents. "This must be Paradise."

"I will first pick the vegetables for Grandmother, and use the compass rose for directions to the distant garden patches."

Standing on the compass rose, she sighted the bean patch. The compass point at her feet was marked E. She walked east.

She picked the beans and put them in the basket. That was easy, beans hung in large clumps.

Then, back to the compass rose.

She looked at the tomato patch and moved her body to face that way. The compass point at her feet was W. She walked west to the tomato patch.

This task was more difficult because most tomatoes were not ripe, and the vines and leaves hid their fruit. She had to search low to the ground and part branches to spot red fruit.

She found four plump, red ripe tomatoes and placed them in the basket.

Next, at the compass rose again, she marked her heading as S, south to the cucumber patch.

She high-stepped through a crazy clutter of cucumber vines trailing wildly on the ground.

Their prickers scratched her bare ankles.

She did not step on the vines.

She soon added three large cucumbers to the basket. Then, she walked north, back to the compass rose.

All vegetables for Grandmother were now in the basket. She placed the basket near the exit arbor gate.

"Yea! Yea! Yea! I did it all by myself, Grandfather!"

She celebrated herself loudly, waving her hands above her head.

"I walked through the garden alone in every direction using the compass rose. Woohoo!"

4

now that I've finished my work for Grandmother, I'm moving on to my adventure in the garden."

Using the compass rose for guidance, Adelyn faced north. Then, she turned her body slowly from north to east to south to west to north again.

At each compass point, she paused to study what was in the garden and what lay beyond, as far as she could see.

"Exactly what an explorer does."

"Buzz, buzz, buzzzzzzzzzz! Whoopee! How ya doin'," Bumblebee said while completing two close flights around her head.

"I'm behind schedule, so I can't visit. Good to see you again. Have a great day."

With a belly laugh, she watched bumbling Bumblebee fly straight away and out of sight.

"Bdltllldlll, hummmmm, bdltlllllltllll,hummm. Who are you?" came a voice.

"I'm Adelyn, a little girl on an adventure. Who are you and where are you?"

"Over here, slurping nectar from a Cardinal Flower. Wait right there. I'll come to you."

"Bdltllldlll, hummmmm, bdltlllllltllll, hummm."

"There, now we can get acquainted," it said, landing on the toe of her lime green sneaker.

24

Adelyn bent over to study the little creature.

"You're a bird!" She exclaimed, noticing its beak, wings, feathers and teeny, tiny feet. "Wow, you are so small. What kind of bird are you?"

"I'm a Ruby Throated Hummingbird. Call me Ruby. We are also called hummers."

Ruby darted a few inches up, hovered, turned, darted and perched on a copper plant label.

Adelyn sat on the stone path, her eyes inches from Ruby's slender beak.

"Where are you going on your adventure?" Ruby inquired.

"This garden."

"Why the garden?"

"Grandfather once told me that it's very important to keep a garden, because a well-tended garden will take care of you.

"He also said it reminds him of the Garden of Eden in the Hebrew Bible, a symbol of life, unity and peace.

"I'm on this adventure to find out what that means."

At that instant, Ruby shot up into the sky, out of sight.

Surprised, Adelyn wondered why Ruby left so suddenly.

Something small and yellow moved in front of her. She lost sight of it and waited, watching.

It moved again, swift, secretly.

"There it is." But Adelyn couldn't lock onto it with her eyes. "I have to get closer."

She tip-toed south and west through the cucumber vines again, until she was close to where the thing had moved, between the tomato patch and the rock wall.

She crouched down, elbows on her knees.

A shrill voice demanded, "Who are you, and what are you looking for?"

"I'm Adelyn, a little girl on an adventure. Who are you and where are you?"

She looked where she was sure she had seen the thing move. She waited, quiet, patient.

A wasp buzzed past her ear and flew straight in front of her. She prepared to swat the stinger, if it came at her again.

Instantly, the wasp stuck, spreadeagled in midair, wobbling, at arm's length before her.

"Wow! What happened to you, Wasp?" Adelyn wondered.

Then, she saw that Wasp was trapped, not moving, in the sticky silk of a large spider web. Her eyes focused on the maze of slender, silky threads hanging vertically. The spiderweb had been invisible to her until Wasp struck it.

"Got it," said the creature with a shrill voice.

A huge, brightly colored, black and yellow spider appeared at the top edge of the web.

Stepping out like a big-bellied acrobat with eight spindly legs, the spider walked swiftly down the web to the wasp.

It wrapped the wasp in spider silk, and then bit the wasp.

"There, now, da wasp will marinate with ma venom fer a while, then I'll eat it."

"Nice polka-dotted hat and, ooooo, I like da lime green sneakahs! What's up with you?"

"Oh, I'm just watching what you're doing," Adelyn answered. "The black and yellow markings on your body are awesome. Would make a great outfit for Halloween."

"I'm Garden Spider. This wasp's ma lunch. Had ta wait a long time fer it ta blunder inta ma web."

"What can I do fer you, Little Girl on an Adventure?" asked Garden Spider, playfully repeating her introduction.

"I'm on this adventure to discover how a well-tended garden takes care of the creatures who live here, or visit the garden."

A shadow crossed the space between Adelyn and the spider.

"Kee-you! ... Kee-you! ... Kee-you! I see you," Hawk said, gliding slowly, high above the garden.

5

S erious adventure you're on," Garden Spider said, while pausing to think about Adelyn's quest. "I can only tell you ma duties an' facts about ma life. Maybe that'll help you."

"Yes. What you've done so far is eye-opening for me."

"There's so much work fer wild creatures ta do day an' night. You watch an' listen, Little Girl on an Adventure. I'll work an' explain ma life."

Garden Spider took the wasp from the center of the web to the back.

"I take what I need from da garden, like every creature who lives here or visits."

Then, Garden Spider started repairing the web, one section at a time.

"Wind, rain, falling sticks an' creatures tore da web ta tatters overnight."

"Can't catch flies with a web full a' holes."

Garden Spider worked and sang a song with a DownEast, Maine accent, in Gregorian chant.

Ah da Gahden Spidah
Grasshoppah
O wicked yum
Ya spit da dark brown yuk
Yum, yum
Ah hop, an leap, an skip

Evar spinnin' da web
Wasp, ya tail-end stingah
Yum da yum
Yip, yip
O me, O mah O
Nip an snip
Ah go
Mosquito, yo needle nose
Wobbly blows
Sticky, shiny threads
Aw in da web
Aphid-adid, yo tiny
Yo yummy plant sapsuckah
O wicked yum da yuk
Ah da Gahden Spidah

The spider's song made her laugh so hard she rolled on her side.

Garden Spider watched her reaction to the song with wonder, then explained the lyrics.

"Insects fly inta da garden an' inta ma web. I catch an' eat 'em by da hundreds all summer long."

"They harm the plants. You're protecting the garden."

She continued watching the spider's patient, skillful snipping, spinning, attaching silk to patch holes in the web.

"Tonight, same as every night, I eat ma web. I spin a new one before sunrise tomorrow."

"And make a new web all over again?"

"Yep. Web silk is great food fer me."

"An' best ta have a fresh-made web ta catch insects the next day, or I'm not doing ma duty. An' I'm not gonna eat."

The spider continued with its story while patching the web.

"Always remember that some spiders can give very nasty bites ta humans an' critters, so it's not wise ta handle 'em."

"Oh yea, like brown recluse and black widow spiders. And snakes. This spring, Grandmother spotted a fat timber rattlesnake under a log."

She warned me, "Never, ever handle a rattler or copperhead. Give them plenty of room. They're poisonous and can kill you."

"Grandmother also said, 'No wild animals are bad. They were created by God, same as us. Each has a duty for Mother Nature.'"

"Smart grandmother ya got. Best mind her. Snakes an' lots a creatures that visit this garden eat da same insects I eat. Life is a competition fer survival. We all have different tools ta get food, build shelter an' defend ourselves."

Garden Spider worked finicky on a silk thread that would not stick. It stuck.

"I'm a female garden spider. I have only one year ta do all ma duties. Male spiders have shorter lives," Garden Spider explained.

"We mate ta have young spiders, but don't live tagether. He lives his life I live mine."

Garden Spider threw out a long silk thread to a high tomato vine, and swung across the web to repair another section.

She continued explaining her life.

"Last October, a female garden spider placed ma egg in a sack with a thousand other spider eggs. She also provided food fer all of us."

"How is that possible? A thousand spider eggs and their food in one sack?"

"Each egg is very small. When da tiny spider hatches, it's a speck a' dust. We hatched before winter, a thousand tiny spiders, but stayed in da egg sack."

"How fun was that?" Adelyn asked.

"It's da spider's life. Better than gettin' eaten by a lizard, shrew or bird," Garden Spider replied.

"When spring came, we thousand itsy bitsy spiders broke out a' da sack ta begin our duties.

"But seven hundred a' those spiders soon became food fer other garden creatures.

"After a female garden spider has placed her eggs in da sack, she's finished all her important work in life, an' she dies.

"Da web is my life. Da garden is my world. I start life here. Do my duties here. My life ends here."

Garden Spider's facts about a spider's life, duty and death revealed something very important to Adelyn.

Recently, Grandmother read to her from the Book of Genesis in the Hebrew Bible. She didn't understand Adam and Eve being cast out of the Garden of Eden and into the world.

Until now.

She told the story to Garden Spider.

"God made Adam and Eve out of clay. He gave them the Garden of Eden to live in. But they disobeyed God's rule not to eat the forbidden fruit. God sent Adam and Eve out of the Garden of Eden.

"After they ate the forbidden fruit, they had knowledge of good and evil. So, they could choose to do whatever they wanted.

"Before that day, Adam and Eve had everything they needed. They were innocent, like all wild creatures. Following instinct was their only way to live.

"Day to day they had food, water, shelter, and companionship. No bad choices no bad actions, simple, good life in nature.

"Then, cast out in the real world, as humans, they had to work for everything they needed. Life was hard. They suffered pain, loss, warfare, injury and illness. That has been life for humans from the peaceful days in the Garden of Eden to today."

Waving her hands over her head excitedly, Adelyn said, "Garden Spider, I think I got it now.

"Your life, my life, and the way of all living things, and non-living things, is our web of life in the Garden of Earth, after Eden.

"Except that wild creatures continue to follow instinct, while humans choose what they will do.

"Bad choices have consequences."

"You can discover meaning. I can't. Fer me, that's not where da story starts or ends," Garden Spider said.

"My egg sack full a' baby spiders is da future."

"I wish you da best with da adventure in da garden. Now, I must get back ta work."

Garden Spider cast a long silk thread into the wind to stick on a fieldstone high in the wall. Then, she swung clean out of sight.

6

Out of the corner of her eye, Adelyn spied something small, flying straight toward her head.

Startled, she flinched and ducked her head.

"Bdltlldlll, hummmmm, bdltllllllltllll, hummm."

"I'm back!"

"Hey! Remember me? It's Ruby," the tiny bird said, now hovering inches from her nose.

"Yes, of course, I remember you, Ruby."

She sat on the stone path to be close to Ruby.

"What happened back there? Why did you fly away after we first met?"

"It's a long story, and never-ending."

She darted up, and over, to perch once again on a nearby copper plant sign.

"Ruby, you have a drop of blood by your eye," she said, leaning forward with deep concern.

Ruby twisted her head and wiped the blood droplet on her wing feathers.

"Battle wound," Ruby said. "Earlier, when I zipped outta here, I had just caught sight of a hummer invading my territory. It was going for the coneflowers next to the grassy path. I got there just in time to scare it off.

"Then, the fun started. That hummer flew to the hummingbird feeder in your grandparents' backyard.

"Flying there at top speed, I find three hummers fighting for my feeder. As soon as I fought off one hummer, another one tried to knock me out.

"Good news: I won the battle. Bad news: I suffered a cut between the eyes.

"If I tell you more about me and my duties in life, will that help you with the garden adventure?"

"For sure, Ruby. I want to know all about your life."

"Okay," Ruby began. "I'm a female hummer. I don't have pretty ruby colored feathers on my throat, like males have. My feathers are drab, which helps me hide from enemies.

"The male hummer and I only get together for mating.

"I'm responsible for most of the work raising hummer chicks.

"Have you cracked open a walnut shell?" Ruby inquired.

"That's an odd question. Yea, why?" Adelyn replied.

"Did a shell sometimes crack open perfectly, giving you two equal half shells?" Ruby asked.

"Oh yea, and I get two big meats, and no hull chips. We crack English walnuts every year at Christmastime."

"Our nests are half a walnut shell," Ruby explained.

Adelyn's eyes went wide open with wonder about the tiny hummingbird's unfolding life story.

"Hummers like to make nests in gardens, like this one. Our food is nearby, and the best materials to build our nests are here.

"I spent the last week building my nest in the clematis vine where you entered the garden.

"Later today, I will lay two eggs in the nest, each the size of a tic tac.

"I sit on the eggs and keep them warm until they hatch in a couple weeks.

"The chicks take their first flights in three weeks, after hatching.

"A month after hatching, they're adults and fly away with full duties as hummers."

"A month! How can they learn so much about life in one month?" Adelyn asked.

Ruby explained, "Hummer chicks are small, only one skinny inch long. I feed them. They grow fast.

"We depend on instinct for survival, like all wild animals. Instinct helps us find the food we need, find mates, build nests, avoid threats and escape danger.

"I eat nectar all day long, because I'm so small and need lots of energy. I fly 30 to 45 miles an hour from flower to flower.

"Has anybody told you how smart hummers are?"

"No, but you're so small," Adelyn noted.

"Don't mix smarts with size," Ruby said, laughing. "Excuse me. I'm not laughing at you. Never thought of my body like that.

"Hummers carve out their own territory, a home base, for food, shelter and nesting, same as other wild creatures.

"We defend ourselves against enemies, like snakes, frogs, and lizards."

Adelyn added, "And other hummers."

"Yea, like the fight I had today," Ruby agreed. "My home base is the size of your grandparents' property.

"Want to know something hummers are really good at?" Ruby asked.

Adelyn said, "The list of great things you do is already long."

Ruby continued, "I know the exact location of every flower in my home base. I keep track of my visits to each flower, so I know when to go back to collect its nectar."

"Absolutely amazing!" Adelyn remarked. "You know every flowering plant in the garden and all around the woods, too?"

"Yep, if it's in my territory. There's more," Ruby said. "Hummers are great pollinators of flowering plants.

"To be fair, bees and butterflies are pollinators, too, but I'm talking up hummers.

"I collect nectar from hundreds of flowers a day. When I slurp the nectar, the pollen from that flower sticks on my forehead and pollinates the next flower I visit.

"And on and on."

"Grandmother said hummers' work is very good for garden plants. You eat harmful insects and spiders."

"Yea, hummers get protein from eating spiders and bugs. I'm getting to like your grandmother."

"I don't like mosquitos," Adelyn said. "Their bites itch like crazy. If I scratch a bite, my skin bleeds. And wasps! I really don't like wasps.

"Last month, I was chasing a soccer ball over there at the forest edge when a huge swarm flew off their nest at me.

"They stung my head everywhere. So painful. I fainted.

"Grandfather saw what happened, picked me up, and carried me to the house.

"Grandmother washed my head with cold, soapy water and ice until the swelling went down."

"Wasp stings are bad news," Ruby agreed. "I must pause the story of my life there.

"Now, I have to fill up with nectar, sit in my nest, watch for enemies, and wait for my eggs to pop out of my body.

"My life, my duties, go on.

"Very soon, there will be two more tiny hummers to feed, care for and protect.

"I wish you all the best with your adventure in the garden. I will watch for your return."

"Thank you. Good luck to you and the chicks."

Ruby blasted straight up and away to slurp nectar.

7

A grasshopper hanging from a stick caught Adelyn's eye. She crouched down, hands on knees, to watch.

Moving up close, she saw that a red ant was carrying the grasshopper, many times its size, down a dead tree branch.

Progress was slow, bouncy and halting.

The ant used its mandibles, like human hands, to hold on to one of the grasshopper's antennae.

She was fascinated.

The ant used tiny claws at the ends of its six legs to hold itself on the stick. It lifted, pulled, and pushed the swaying grasshopper.

Progress was slow and hard work, but the ant didn't seem to care about troubles. Its job was to get the grasshopper down the branch.

The ant stopped to look ahead to where it was taking the grasshopper.

Four more red ants climbed onto the stick and went straight to the first ant that was struggling with the grasshopper.

All five ants worked now as a team to move the grasshopper down the branch.

The five ants formed two teams. Two ants took over the job of holding the grasshopper by one of its legs. Three ants cut up the grasshopper.

They carried the legs and other body parts down the stick to the stone path, ate the grasshopper's edible parts and disappeared down a burrow.

"Humm!" Adelyn was amused, puzzled. "The ants didn't talk to each other, but they definitely worked well together.

"Some of their head and body movements might be gestures to coordinate their work.

"Maybe they use sign language?

"It's amazing how five ants came together to bring that big grasshopper to their underground nest.

"Wonder how many grasshoppers it takes to feed a nest of ants for one day?"

She made a mental note, "Ants, great adventure for another day!"

"Something's watching me." She had experienced this odd feeling on the forest path.

"All right, who are you, and where are you?" No answer.

She stood up and slowly turned around to her right, inspecting the garden.

Nothing.

She turned around to her left, studying the garden, again.

Nothing.

She was looking at the exit arbor gate, when she noticed something about the stone threshold was different.

Then, she made out a furry creature sitting, patient, with a long bushy tail, brown eyes, black nose, and tall reddish ears—staring at her.

"Yip, yip. You found me, Little Girl on an Adventure in the Garden. How do you do? I'm Reynard Gray Fox. Call me Reynard."

"How do you know me, Reynard?"

"I have been sitting here the whole time," Reynard said, while continuously looking around.

"Watched you walk the path with the basket from your grandparents' house. Pick veggies. Heard your introduction to creatures."

Adelyn walked to the exit arbor, stopping where she had placed the wicker basket earlier. Reynard was sitting only a few steps away.

"You won't harm me, will you?"

"I was just about to ask you the same question, Little Girl on an Adventure in the Garden."

"Wild animals fear humans. We would much rather fight our natural enemies."

"Maybe Reynard has lots to tell about animals fearing humans," Adelyn mused. She made another mental note, "Why do animals fear humans? A new adventure, but not now."

"Reynard, mind if I sit next to you on the stone?"

"Certainly not."

"So, you overheard why I'm on an adventure in the garden?"

"Yep. From your grandfather, you learned that a well-tended garden takes care of creatures who live in or visit the garden.

"Your grandfather also said that a garden is a symbol of life, unity and peace, as in the biblical Garden of Eden."

"Wow, you've got a great memory, Reynard."

"That may be so, but just what those words mean about the garden, you will have to figure out for yourself."

"I'm only a fox, depending on instinct for what to do in nature. Not finding meaning."

"That's exactly what Crow said with, 'See more. Do more. Know more,'" Adelyn recalled.

"What's a crow got to do with it?" Reynard asked.

"I'm so sorry, my mind was wandering," she apologized.

"Speaking as one creature, a gray fox, I can only tell you about my life. Maybe that will help you unravel the mystery surrounding the garden."

"Yes," Adelyn said.

"I'm a male gray fox. The female fox is Vixen. We mate and stay together for years to raise our young, the kits, year after year.

"We hunt food together, all kinds of small creatures. Mice, rabbits, frogs, birds, earthworms.

"We keep our den together.

"Vixen gave birth to our three kits a few weeks ago. Now, I hunt food for the whole family.

"She stays in the den nursing and protecting the kits, until they're at least three months old."

"That's kinda like our family life, Reynard," Adelyn offered.

"Perhaps."

Reynard continued, "After sunrise this morning, I killed a wild turkey jake. Cached most of it under a rock, and brought a leg and thigh to Vixen."

"What do you mean you 'cached most of it under a rock?'" Adelyn asked.

"Vixen and I can't eat a whole turkey in one meal," Reynard explained. "And we cannot have leftover food where Vixen and the kits stay. Food odors will tell our enemies where our den is.

"I buried most of it in the cool dirt, under that rock. Took part of it back to the den."

Reynard pointed his nose to a huge boulder by the garden entrance arbor.

"Like our fridge," Adelyn said.

"Maybe," Reynard offered. "I have free time now, because I cached enough food for two days. But I must stay near the den and keep watch in case there's danger.

"Last week, a pack of coyotes discovered our previous den that was a long way from here."

"What are coyotes, Reynard?"

"Imagine a big gray, wild dog," Reynard explained. "They mate for life, are clever hunters and have large territories.

"Foxes compete with coyotes for the same food. But they are so much bigger than we are.

"And they sometimes hunt in packs. It's very hard for a fox to survive an attack from a pack of coyotes."

Reynard continued the story about the coyotes' discovery of their den. "So, one day last week, when I was hunting, Vixen discovered the coyotes searching for our den.

"In the knick of time, she carried the kits to this den, one by one, and saved them.

"That's why Vixen must stay in the den with the kits while I hunt for food. Kits can't defend themselves.

"We set up several dens in our territory as protection against enemies. Discovered at one den, we move to another den, especially when the kits arrive.

"See my paw? Our claws are sharp. We can move 'em in an' out, like a cat's paw.

"A gray fox can climb trees to pick fruit, catch animals for food, and escape danger.

"You must face extreme danger from your enemies all of the time?" Adelyn remarked.

"Same as all wild animals. Life's tough. Hard. There are no guarantees," Reynard answered.

"We feed, care for and protect our own. But if an enemy threatens us, like the coyotes last week, we move the den to a safe place.

"If we can't flee, we fight for our lives.

"When an enemy threatens her kits, Vixen becomes a vicious, formidable demon.

"She's an extreme four-legged fiend. Sharp fangs and claws. Muscles of spring steel.

"Enemies don't want to go up against Vixen. "It's my duty to fight by her side.

"The kits are our future as gray foxes. We will defend each other and our kits to the last breath."

"That's serious," Adelyn stated.

"Yep," Reynard replied. "It's the truth about life in the real world."

"After the Garden of Eden," Adelyn completed Reynard's sentence in a whisper.

At once, Reynard jumped to his feet and raced to the forest.

"He must have heard or smelled something," Adelyn guessed. Then she asked herself, "How does my well-tended garden take care of me, and all the things that live here?"

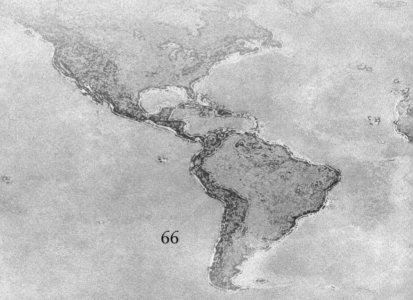

She took a deep breath and let it out slowly.
Again. Calmed, her thoughts flow freely in prayer.

Garden of Earth

Day by day God's miraculous web of life,
Fertile plain of my birth,
You give me food and shelter,
Liberty springs from my soul,
I dream of goodness for all,
Courage to fight for the right cause,
Love without question family and friends,
Create things needed, beautiful, fun,
Grow older, see more, do more, know more,
Bear children, raise them good and just.
Hard living wild creatures and humans,
When our life-work is finished, we die.
Let us be worthy, for God's afterlife awaits us.

"Wild creatures of the garden are gifted with instinct for survival. Each kind of animal does its duty in the world.

"God gave humans the freedom to choose what to do.

"Make good choices, and good things follow.

"Make a poor choice or a terrible choice, and the outcome is our fault. We don't act on instinct. And there's nothing and no one else to blame. A bad decision can harm other people, property, the earth, and more.

"But I'm confused about competition among wild animals and humans.

"And the female creatures have a lot of responsibility for raising their young.

"And I see life everywhere, but what about unity and peace?

"I'll ask Grandfather and Grandmother to explain.

"The winding stone path is our walk through life.

"Guidance from the Bible, Constitution, other writings and good persons, like our parents, grandparents and friends, helps us lead a good life.

"That's our moral compass!

"Our duty is to obey God's Ten Commandments, follow man-made laws, be true to ourselves, love and respect others and care for nature.

"Humans till, plant and harvest from the Garden of Earth. We keep healthy its creatures, plants, soil, water and air. And ourselves, too. The Garden of Earth takes care of us and all living things.

"Still, humans are not perfect.

"We will make mistakes. When bad things happen, we must do our best to right the wrongs and make our world better."

Hawk's shadow crossed the exit arbor gate.

"Kee-you! . . . Kee-you! . . . Kee-you!" It screeched and continued soaring above the garden.

70

But Hawk didn't say anything else.

"Adelyn, where are you?"

"Grandmother and Grandfather!" Adelyn said, feeling like she suddenly awoke from a dream. "Here I am. On my way, now."

Her grandparents were walking the grassy path to the entrance arbor gate, holding hands and smiling.

"Wait there for me."

She grabbed the basket of vegetables and ran back along the stone path.

At the entrance gate, Grandfather picked her up with his big, calloused hands and lifted her head deep into the clematis flowers.

"Oh Grandfather and Grandmother! I had a wonderful adventure in the garden!"

"You must have. It's past noon," Grandmother said, laughing.

"Wait till I tell you what happened!"

"In the basket are the veggies I picked for you, Grandmother."

"And Grandfather, I used the compass rose to explore all over the garden."

"We're so proud of you," Grandfather said. "Lunch is on the table," Grandfather continued.

"Let's walk back to the house, while you tell us all about your adventure in the garden."

Adelyn told her grandparents about the creatures she met in the garden.

She told and retold how the garden takes care of all wild creatures and humans.

Until she fell fast asleep on her pillow.

CAST OF CHARACTERS FOR
ADELYN'S ADVENTURE IN THE GARDEN

To Young Readers:

Use the cast of characters to retell the story of *Adelyn's Adventure in the Garden.*

Make use of these characters to create a new adventure anywhere.

What do you imagine will happen in *Adelyn's Adventure on the Beach*?

Share the book and your stories with friends. Have fun adventuring every day.

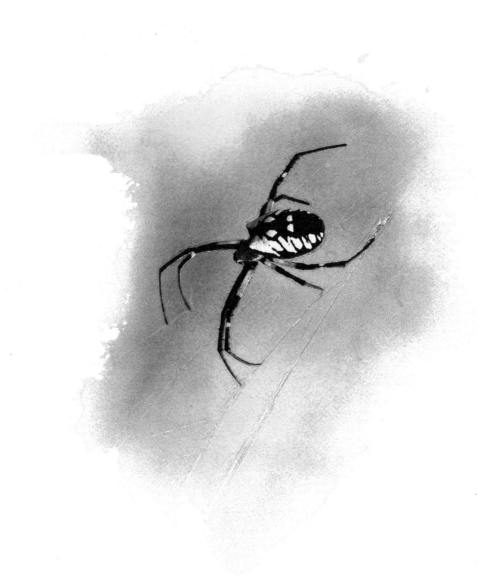

BOOK TYPEFACES

Adelyn's Adventure is a storybook series for children of all ages. The author created the imaginative concept and design.

Skia typeface

The genesis for this typeface was a 1st century BC stone carving of Greek writing. Skia, translated to English, is "shadow." Matthew Carter created its modern form for Apple Computer in 1994. Skia, of ancient origin, is a perfect typeface to launch Adelyn's Adventure.

Helvetica Neue typeface

Developed in 1957, this is a balanced, neutral typeface of Swiss and German design. It is technically well-suited to business concerns. Helvetica Neue is used here to relate book publication details.

Papyrus typeface

Chris Costello created this typeface in 1982. He drew it by hand drawn during a period of six months with calligraphy pen on textured paper. Costello wanted to create a typeface that would show what ancient scriptures would look like if written in English with Latin characters. Papyrus typeface is aesthetically pleasing and perfect for wisdom quotes.

Luminari typeface

An ornate, mysterious style of writing with deep roots in the ninth through fifteenth centuries, the High Middle Ages, Luminari is used for the first letter of the first word of each chapter.

Cochin typeface

Selected for the narrative, Cochin gets its name from Charles Nicolas Cochin (1715 – 1790), a French copper engraver. Cochin typeface is unique, stylish and historical—well suited for a children's story.

ABOUT THE AUTOR

CHARLES BRUCKERHOFF started life in Augusta, Missouri, in 1947, on a small farm near The Big Muddy. He spent many days exploring the hills, valleys, fields and streams of the Ozark Mountain foothills.

At 19, he joined the United States Army and served in Vietnam. Returning to the USA in 1969, he went to college, studying English, literature, philosophy and research methods. In 1995, he created a firm, Curriculum Research and Evaluation, Inc. (www.creus.com), focused on the social and cultural life of children living in poverty. He believes the best way to gain personal knowledge, social skills, moral behavior, spirituality, and healing for children and adults is through the real world, out the back door with friends.

Currently, Charles works as the author and publisher of Adelyn's Adventure Series for Sequoia House Books. He also devotes time to shepherding the firm, now run by his lovely wife, Theresa, and to family life with four sons, five grandchildren, friends, and neighbors. His hobbies include community service, artisan bread baking, gardening, traditional quilting, and studying American history, ancient civilizations of the world, the Hebrew Bible and the New Testament. He places no limit on new adventures.

Sequoia House Books™

When the author visited Kings Canyon National Park in California, he came upon The Fallen Monarch among the Sierra Redwoods of Grant Grove. This giant tree was hollowed out by countless forest fires before falling to the forest floor hundreds of years ago. These trees live for 3,000 years or more, and can reach heights of 300 feet and trunk diameters of 30 feet.

Native American Indians dwelt in the region for 5,000 years. The Monaches tribe, lived in Kings Canyon, keeping their villages yearlong in the Sierra Nevada foothills, and summering in the redwood forests. The Fallen Monarch was used as a temporary "house" from 1868 to 1878 and as a stable by the US Cavalry from 1890 to 1914.

After its initial discovery by Europeans in 1794, botanists argued over what to name this magnificent and gargantuan species of conifer. Eventually, they chose Sequoia, in honor of a Cherokee man, "Sequoyah," for his enormously important achievement, in 1821, of creating an alphabet for the Cherokee language. The noblest of trees in the world are thus named in honor of a Native American genius of Cherokee descent.

Sequoia House Books™ publishes original literature that imparts knowledge to children, inspiring them to be the best they can be and preparing them to help make the world a better place for all living things.

SHB

CPSIA information can be obtained
at www.ICGtesting.com
Printed in the USA
BVHW022102021022
648494BV00006B/50